Peter Piper

AND OTHER BUSY-TIME RHYMES

Illustrated by

KRISTA BRAUCKMANN-TOWNS

JANE CHAMBLESS WRIGHT

WENDY EDELSON

ANITA NELSON

LORI NELSON FIELD

DEBBIE PINKNEY

KAREN PRITCHETT

PUBLICATIONS INTERNATIONAL, LTD.

PETER PIPER

Peter Piper picked a peck
    Of pickled peppers;
A peck of pickled peppers
    Peter Piper picked.

If Peter Piper picked a peck
    Of pickled peppers,
Where's the peck of pickled peppers
    Peter Piper picked?

OLD WOMAN, OLD WOMAN

There was an old woman
    Tossed up in a basket,
Nineteen times as high as the moon.
    Where was she going?
I couldn't but ask it,
    For in her hand she carried a broom.
Old woman, old woman,
    Old woman, said I,
O whither, O whither,
    O whither, so high?
To brush the cobwebs off the sky!
    And I'll be back again by and by.

WILLY BOY

Willy boy, Willy boy,
    Where are you going?
I will go with you,
    If that I may.

I'm going to the meadow
    To see them a-mowing;
I'm going to help them
    To make the hay.

THE OLD WOMAN
OF LEEDS

There was an old woman of Leeds,
   Who spent her time in good deeds.
She worked for the poor
   Till her fingers were sore,
This pious old woman of Leeds!

JACK

All work and no play
   Makes Jack a dull boy.
All play and no work
   Makes Jack a mere toy.

OLD CHAIRS

If I'd as much money as I could spend,
    I never would cry old chairs to mend.
Old chairs to mend, old chairs to mend,
    I never would cry old chairs to mend.
If I'd as much money as I could tell,
    I never would cry old clothes to sell.
Old clothes to sell, old clothes to sell,
    I never would cry old clothes to sell.

SWEEP

Sweep, sweep, chimney sweep,
  From the bottom to the top.
Sweep it all up, chimney sweep,
  From the bottom to the top.

SHOPPING ROBINS

A robin and a robin's son
 Once went to town to buy a bun.
They could not decide
 On plum or plain,
And so they went back home again.

TUB, TUB, TUB

The old woman stands
    At the tub, tub, tub,
The dirty clothes to rub, rub, rub.
    But when they are clean,
And fit to be seen,
    She'll dress like a lady
And dance on the green.

TO MARKET

To market, to market, to buy a fat pig,
  Home again, home again, jiggety-jig.
To market, to market, to buy a fat hog,
  Home again, home again, jiggety-jog.